firecrackers

spring couplets

富贵有余年年平

花开四季月月香

decorated kumquat tree

broom

whole fish

gong

spring lantern

春

THIS IS A BORZOI BOOK PUBLISHED BY ALFRED A. KNOPF

Copyright © 2008 by Grace Lin
All rights reserved.
Published in the United States by Alfred A. Knopf, an imprint of Random House
Children's Books, a division of Random House, Inc., New York.

KNOPF, BORZOI BOOKS, and the colophon are registered trademarks of Random House, Inc.
www.randomhouse.com/kids
Educators and librarians, for a variety of teaching tools, visit us at
www.randomhouse.com/teachers

Library of Congress Cataloging-in-Publication Data
Lin, Grace.
Bringing in the New Year / Grace Lin.
p. cm.
Summary: A Chinese American family prepares for and celebrates the Lunar New Year.
End notes discuss the customs and traditions of Chinese New Year.
ISBN 978-0-375-83745-6 (trade) — ISBN 978-0-375-93745-3 (lib. bdg.)
[1. Chinese New Year—Fiction. 2. Chinese Americans—Fiction.] I. Title.
PZ7.L644Br 2008
[E]—dc22
2007011687

The illustrations in this book were created using Turner Design Gouache
on Arches hot-press paper.

MANUFACTURED IN CHINA

January 2008

10 9 8 7 6 5 4

To my niece Lily,
who I hope continues to bring
in every New Year smiling

Bringing In the NEW YEAR

新年快樂

Grace Lin

ALFRED A. KNOPF
NEW YORK

Is the New Year coming?
I hope so!
We try to welcome it in.

So, Jie-Jie
sweeps the old
year out of the house.

福

Ba-Ba hangs the
spring-happiness poems.

Ma-Ma makes the
get-rich dumplings.

Mei-Mei gets a fresh haircut.

And I put on my new *qi pao* dress for the New Year feast. Now will the New Year come?

Pop! Pop! Pop!
Do you hear the firecrackers?
Are they bringing in the New Year?

No! But they brought in the lions. They're here to scare away last year's bad luck.

They scare Mei-Mei too.
Don't cry, Mei-Mei!

Where is the New Year?
We carry the lanterns to light its way.

I hope the New Year
follows us soon.

Look, there's the dragon!
Auntie is waking him up by opening his eyes.
The New Year must be coming.

Yes, hooray!
The New Year is here!
Happy New Year,
everyone!

The dragon's awake!
Is it the New Year at last?

Chinese New Year, which is now more commonly called Lunar New Year (since it is based on the lunar calendar and many other countries besides China observe it), is one of the most celebrated holidays in the world. It is such an important festival that it traditionally lasted for fifteen days, ending with the Lantern Festival. Nowadays, however, most people just celebrate for one day. It is a time for families and friends to get together and is the biggest, most exciting event of the year.

There are many customs and traditions associated with the New Year. People prepare for this festival for almost a month ahead of time. Houses are cleaned (to sweep away the old year), debts are paid (so the New Year begins without obligation), and red decorations featuring spring poems and good wishes are put up to welcome in the New Year (red is considered a lucky color). People also prepare themselves—cutting their hair and buying new clothes. All this is done so the New Year can start fresh.

To make sure that the New Year is full of plenty of food and luck, people feast at New Year banquets. Most foods have symbolic meanings—oranges, dumplings, and a whole fish mean wealth, and eating them brings prosperity into the New Year. To scare away evil spirits, firecrackers are lit and lions are given offerings (usually lucky red envelopes of money) to dance. The bad spirits are also frightened by the bright lanterns, which light the way for the New Year.

And no New Year is complete without the appearance of the lucky dragon. When a new dragon is used for a parade, it can be "woken up" by an eye opening ceremony. This simple ceremony paints in the eyes of the dragon so he can see the symbolic sun (the round shape carried by the parade leader). The dragon chases the sun around and around, ensuring that we will have many nights and days. His chase is accompanied by many merrymakers, whose joyous noise helps scare any remaining evil spirits, guaranteeing a happy, lucky New Year!

good luck sign

bunny lantern

red envelope

drum

dumplings

symbolic sun

qi pao

oranges

noisemaker